THIS BOOK
BELONGS TO:

For Anna
M.W.

For Sebastian,
David & Candlewick
H.O.

Published by arrangement with Walker Books Ltd, London

Dual language edition first published 2006 by Mantra Lingua
Global House, 303 Ballards Lane, London N12 8NP
http://www.mantralingua.com

Text copyright © 1991 Martin Waddell
Illustrations copyright © 1991 Helen Oxenbury
Dual language text & audio copyright © 2006 Mantra Lingua
This edition 2013

Printed in Hatfield UK FP130613PB07130351

البطَّةُ المزارِعةُ

FARMER DUCK

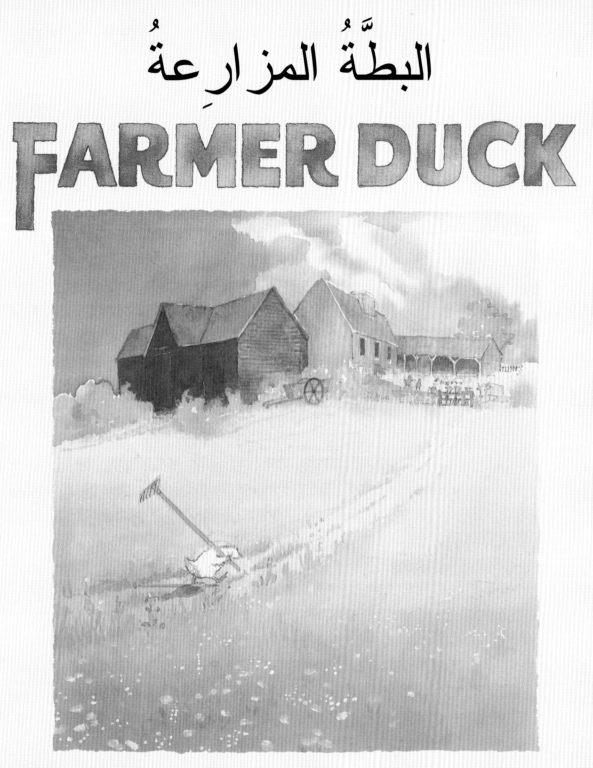

written by
MARTIN WADDELL

illustrated by
HELEN OXENBURY

Mantra Lingua

كانَ هُناكَ فيما مَضى بَطَّةٌ مِن سوءِ حَظِّها أَنْ تَعيشَ مَعَ
مُزارِعٍ عَجوزٍ كَسْلانَ.
كانَتِ الْبَطَّةُ هي التي تَقومُ بِأَعْمالِ الْمَزْرَعَةِ
والْمُزارِعُ يَبْقى طولَ الْيَوْمِ في سَريرِهِ.

There once was a duck who had the bad luck
to live with a lazy old farmer.
The duck did the work.
The farmer stayed
all day in bed.

كانَتِ الْبَطَّةُ تُحْضِرُ الْبَقَرَةَ مِنَ الْحَقْلِ.

وكانَ الْمُزارِعُ يُنادي: "كَيْفَ الْعَمَلُ مَعَكِ؟"

فَكانَتِ الْبَطَّةُ تَرُدُّ: "كواك!"

The duck fetched the cow from the field.
"How goes the work?" called the farmer.
The duck answered,
"Quack!"

كانَتِ الْبَطَّةُ تُحْضِرُ الْغَنَماتِ من التَّلِّ.

وكانَ الْمَزارِعُ يُنادي: "كَيْفَ الْعَمَلُ مَعَكِ؟"

فَكانَتِ الْبَطَّةُ تَرُدُّ: "كواك!"

The duck brought the sheep from the hill.
"How goes the work?" called the farmer.
The duck answered,
"Quack!"

كانَتِ الْبَطَّةُ تَسوقُ الدَّجاجاتِ إلى كوخِها.
وَكانَ الْمُزارِعُ يُنادي: "كَيْفَ الْعَمَلُ مَعَكِ؟"
فَكانَتِ الْبَطَّةُ تَرُدُّ: "كواك!"

The duck put the hens in their house.
"How goes the work?"
called the farmer.
The duck answered,
"Quack!"

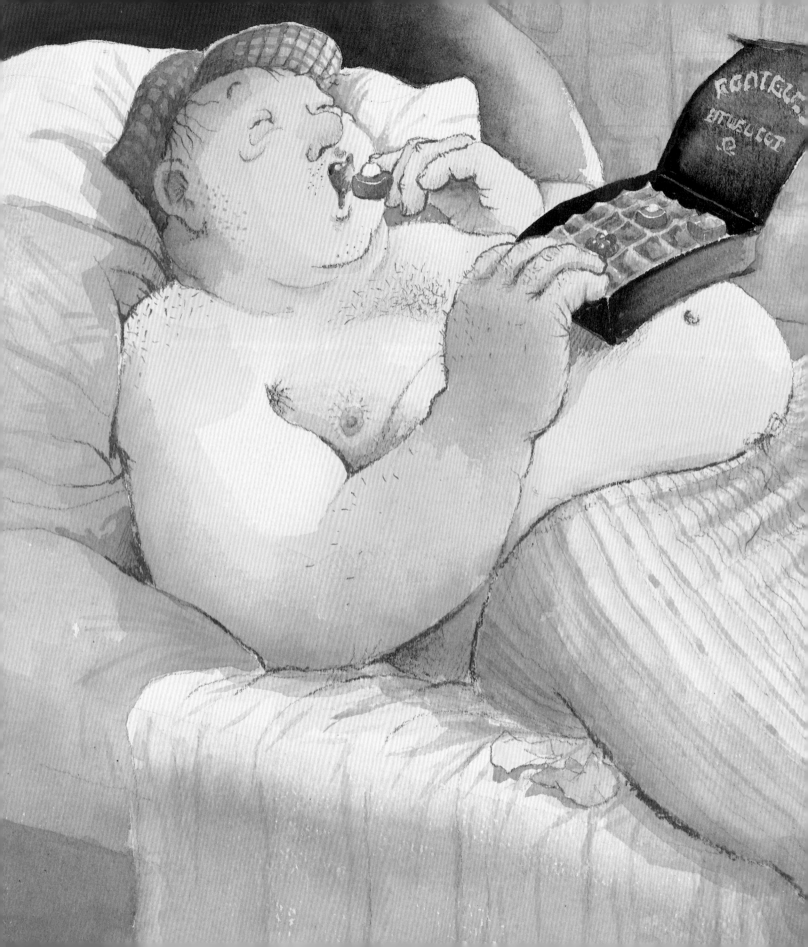

وأَصْبَحَ الْمُزارِعُ بَديناً مِنْ كُثْرَةِ الْبَقاءِ في سَريرِهِ
واسْتاءَتِ الْبَطَّةُ مِنَ الْعَمَلِ طولَ اليَوْمِ.

The farmer got fat through staying in bed
and the poor duck got fed up
with working all day.

"كَيْفَ الْعَمَلُ مَعَكِ؟"

"كواك!"

"How goes the work?"
"QUACK!"

"كَيْفَ الْعَمَلُ مَعَكِ؟"

"كواك!"

"How goes the work?"
"QUACK!"

"كَيْفَ الْعَمَلُ مَعَكِ؟"

"كواك!"

"How goes the work?"
"QUACK!"

"كَيْفَ الْعَمَلُ مَعَكِ؟"

"كواك!"

"How goes the work?"
"QUACK!"

"كَيْفَ الْعَمَلُ مَعَكِ؟"

"كواك!"

"How goes the work?"
"QUACK!"

"كَيْفَ الْعَمَلُ مَعَكِ؟"

"كواك!"

"How goes the work?"
"QUACK!"

فَأَصْبَحَتِ الْبَطَّةُ الْمَسْكِينَةُ نَعْسَانَةً
وَدَامِعَةً وتَعْبَانَةً.

The poor duck was sleepy
and weepy
and tired.

واسْتَاءَتِ الدَّجَاجَاتُ وَالْبَقَرَةُ وَالْغَنَمَاتُ لِأَنَّهَا كَانَتْ تُحِبُّ الْبَطَّةَ،
فَاجْتَمَعَتْ تَحْتَ ضَوْءِ الْقَمَرِ وَدَبَّرَتْ خِطَّةً لِتُنَفِّذَهَا فِي الصَّبَاحِ.

"موو!" قالَتِ الْبَقَرَةُ.
"باء!" قالَتِ الْغَنَمَاتُ.
"كلاك!" قالَتِ الدَّجَاجَاتُ.
وها هِيَ الْخِطَّةُ!

The hens and the cow
and the sheep got very
upset.
They loved the duck.
So they held a meeting
under the moon and
they made a plan
for the morning.

"MOO!" said the cow.
"BAA!" said the sheep.
"CLUCK!" said the hens.
And THAT was the plan!

كانَ قُبَيْلَ الْفَجَرِ وكانَتْ ساحَةُ الْمَزْرَعَةِ لا تَزالُ ساكِنَةً.
فَتَسَلَّلَتِ الْبَقَرَةُ والْغَنَماتُ والدَّجاجاتُ إلى بَيْتِ
الْمُزارِعِ مِنْ خِلالِ الْبابِ الْخَلْفيِّ.

It was just before dawn and the farmyard was still.
Through the back door and into the house
crept the cow and the sheep and the hens.

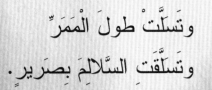

وتَسَلَّتْ طولَ الْمَمَرِّ
وتَسَلَّقَتِ السَّلالِمَ بِصَريرٍ.

They stole down the hall.
They creaked
up the stairs.

ثُمَّ احْتَشَدَتْ تَحْتَ سَرير الْمُزارع وأَخَذَتْ تَتَلَوّى.
بَدَأَ السَّريرُ يَهْتَزُّ فاسْتَيْقَظَ الْمُزارعُ وصرَخَ:
"كَيْفَ الْعَمَلُ مَعَكِ؟"
فَـ . . .

They squeezed under the bed of
the farmer and wriggled about.
The bed started to rock and the
farmer woke up, and he called,
"How goes the work?"
and...

"موو!"

"باء!"

"كلاك!"

"MOO!"
"BAA!"
"CLUCK!"

ورَفَعَتْ الْحَيَواناتُ سَريرَ الْمُزارِعِ الْعَجوزِ
وهَزَّتْهُ ويَصْرَخُ الْمُزارِعُ كَالطَّاووسِ
وزَلْزَلَتْهُ مِنَ الْيَمينِ والْيَسيرِ
إلى أَنْ وقَعَ مِنَ السَّريرِ. . .

They lifted his bed and he started to shout, and they banged
and they bounced the old farmer about and about and about,
right out of the bed...

فَهَرَبَ مَعَ الْبَقَرَةِ وَالْغَنَمَاتِ وَالدَّجاجاتِ
وهي تَخورُ وتَثْغي وتُوَقْوِقُ حَوالَيْهِ.

and he fled with the cow and the sheep and the
hens mooing and baaing and clucking around him.

طولَ الطَّريقِ الْمُنْحَدِرَةِ . . .
"موو!"

Down the lane...
"Moo!"

عَبْرَ الْحُقولِ العَريضَةِ . . .
"باء!"

through the fields...
"Baa!"

فَوْقَ التَّلِّ الْكَبيرِ. . .
"كلاك!"

over the hill...
"Cluck!"

ولَمْ يَرْجَعْ أَبَداً.

and he never came back.

استَيْقَظَتِ الْبَطَّةُ وتَهادَتْ مُرْهَقَةً إلى
ساحَةِ الْمَزْرَعَةِ وهي تَنْتَظِرُ سماعَ:
"كَيْفَ الْعَمَلُ مَعَك؟"
لكِنْ لَمْ يَتَكَلَّمْ أَحَدٌ!

The duck awoke and waddled wearily into the yard expecting
to hear, "How goes the work?"
But nobody spoke!

ثُمَّ رَجِعَتِ الْبَقَرَةُ وَالْغَنَمَاتُ وَالدَّجَاجَاتُ.

"كواك؟" سَأَلَتِ الْبَطَّةُ.

"موو!" خَارَتِ الْبَقَرَةُ.

"باء!" ثَغَتِ الْغَنَمَاتُ.

"كلاك!" وَقْوَقَتِ الدَّجَاجَاتُ.

وَهكذا فَهِمَتِ الْبُطَّةُ الْقِصَّةَ كُلَّها.

Then the cow and the sheep and the
hens came back.
"Quack?" asked the duck.
"Moo!" said the cow.
"Baa!" said the sheep.
"Cluck!" said the hens.
Which told the duck
the whole story.

ثُمَّ أَخَذَتْ تَعْمَلُ جَمِيعًا في مَزْرَعَتِها
وهي تَخورُ وتَثغي وتُوَقْوِقُ.

Then mooing and baaing
and clucking and quacking
they all set to work
on their farm.

Here are some other bestselling

dual language books from Mantra

Lingua for you to enjoy.